Not a Country Kid

Story by Janeen Brian

Illustrations by Alisha Monnin

Contents

Chapter 1	Farewell, Taco	5
Chapter 2	The Farm	9
Chapter 3	Three Lambs	17
Chapter 4	Hero	24
Chapter 5	An Escape!	29
Chapter 6	A Rescue	38
Chapter 7	Mum's Surprise	44

Chapter 1

Farewell, Taco

Finn held out the scrappy dog lead to Mrs Abara. Choking back a sob, he said, "Taco will probably need a new lead. He's chewed this one a bit." Finn attempted a laugh, but none came.

Mrs Abara patted Finn's shoulder. "You know I love Taco, don't you? I will take him for walks. I will sing to him. I will show him your picture." She pointed to a photo on her living room shelf. It was of Finn and Taco. Taco's fur shone golden in the sunlight. "I will keep him happy, Finn. No need to take him to a dog shelter." She nodded kindly. "You travel well. And you make a happy new home with your mama. Maybe later, we can phone or make a video call."

Finn dropped to his knees and wrapped his arms around his pet cocker spaniel. Taco gazed up at him.

"I love you, Taco," Finn said, tears trickling down his cheeks. "Don't forget me, will you?" Blinking hard, he muttered his thanks and said goodbye to Mrs Abara.

His eyes blurring, Finn rushed back to his apartment next door and burst out crying.

"Oh, Finn." His mother hurried towards him from the kitchen and gave him a hug. "I'm sorry."

"I know," Finn said, his breath catching. "But the look in his eyes, Mum. The way he looked at me!"

Finn's mum wiped strands of light brown hair off his cheeks, now damp with grief. "Come on," she said gently. "Let's have something to eat, and then we'll do the last-minute checking of passports and so on."

Finn struggled to eat even the smallest portion of chicken schnitzel and salad, his favourite meal. And later that night, his sleep was ragged with dreams.

The next morning, they tidied and cleaned the apartment. Finn glanced at Mrs Abara's place, hoping he might see Taco through the window, but the curtains were closed.

On their way to the airport, Finn stared out the taxi window as the city traffic rushed past. It felt as if his school and friends were being swept away as well.

And everywhere he looked, there were dog owners walking or running with their pets. Finn bit down on his trembling lip.

Occasionally, his mum caught his eye and smiled encouragingly. "I know how you feel, Finn," she'd said a while back, when she had explained her plan for them to move back to her home country. "But the cost to get a pet across to New Zealand is a lot more than we can afford. It's over a thousand dollars. And then there's the extra cost to get Taco housed while he's quarantined for about ten days. It's just not possible."

Finn's heart dropped at his mum's words. He knew money couldn't appear like magic in a bank account.

Chapter 2

The Farm

As the plane landed in New Zealand, Finn's mum gripped his hand. Her face sparkled. Her dream to return to her homeland had come true. But what about Finn? What was it going to be like living with his mum's older brother, Uncle Rob, while his mum stayed in the city? Finn knew she had to sort out a job, a house and a car, but he'd never even met his uncle.

They had spoken briefly on the phone, but Uncle Rob refused to video call. "Give me sheep over technology, any day," he had said. "My hands are for farming, not for pressing fiddly buttons while staring at a screen."

At the airport entrance, Finn's mum pointed out the Māori carvings. Then, as they collected their luggage, she said, "Uncle Rob … he's … well, it's good of him to have you."

"How long will I be staying with him?" asked Finn, hitching his backpack onto his shoulders. His head buzzed with anxious thoughts.

"Not long," said his mum, vaguely. Then she exclaimed, "There he is! Uncle Rob. Wave, Finn."

But Finn had only seen a small photo of the man. For a moment, he wasn't sure who to wave to. Finally, he saw a man about his mum's age waving back at them.

Outside the airport, Finn and his mum hugged. Finn swallowed hard.

"Thanks again, Rob," Finn's mum said to his uncle. "Love you, Finn. Be good. I'll phone, and I'll come for you as soon as everything's settled. Okay?"

"Goodbye, Mum," Finn said. She hugged him again before she went.

"We've got a bit of a drive ahead of us," said Uncle Rob, heaving himself into a dusty truck with an open back. "I suppose you ate something on the plane?"

"I'm all right, thanks," said Finn, pressing a hand against his stomach to stop the grumbling noise.

Three hours later, they swung into a long driveway. After they'd brought in the luggage, Uncle Rob pointed towards an open door. "That's your room," he said. "Drop your things in there, and I'll throw some meat and veg together for dinner. I don't do fancy food, as it's just me. I cook plain."

The house was full of old furniture, and it smelt stale and musty, especially Finn's bedroom. He was filled with homesickness.

"Righto," said Uncle Rob after dinner, "here we do dishes, so grab that tea towel over there. Then it's goodnight for both of us. We have to be up early. It's lambing time, so we have to check on the mothers and any newborn lambs. And since there's no school for you yet, you can help out around the farm. I hope you've got decent boots, not just those flip-floppy shoes you're wearing."

Finn woke just after sunrise. His eyes roamed about the unfamiliar room, while from the open window came a mixture of sounds. Sheep *baaing* and cows *mooing* like foghorns, and the wind swishing through trees. There was also a clatter of dishes coming from the kitchen. Was he supposed to shower before breakfast? Finn decided to dress near the window, his face puckering at the farm smells from outside.

"Morning," said Uncle Rob, as Finn walked into the kitchen. "There's cereal and toast on the table. Help yourself. I've had mine."

"I'm over here," his uncle called later, when Finn stepped outside. Uncle Rob was feeding two lean, furry border collie dogs that danced about with bright, eager eyes. "Meet Butch and Mack. Mack's the one with a white nose."

At the sight of the dogs, Finn forgot about the pongy smells of the farmyard. He hurried closer, smiling, with his hand out.

"Stop! Not too close." Uncle Rob's tone was urgent and firm. "They're working dogs, not playthings. Remember that." He whistled and cried out, "In the back!" The dogs bounded into the rear of the truck.

"Hop in." Uncle Rob nodded to Finn. "We're going to the lambing paddock."

As the truck bumped along the track, Finn looked at the hills and cloudy sky. His mind struggled to take everything in: the uncle who had not once called him by his name, the dogs he wasn't allowed to pat, the stinky smells and the lack of traffic noise.

But most of all, Finn's heart ached for Taco.

The truck lurched and then stopped. "Over there!" cried Uncle Rob, wrenching the truck door open. "There are a couple of lambs. But something's wrong with the mother!"

Chapter 3

Three Lambs

Finn raced after his uncle as he turned and whistled a command to the dogs. With a bark and a flash of tails, the animals leapt out of the truck and bounded through the gate towards the field.

Finn had never seen so many sheep, and such fat ones at that, together in one spot.

"This is where I keep the ewes who are going to give birth," Uncle Rob shouted. "But I need to get that distressed ewe away from the others." He whistled again and shouted other commands to the dogs.

"Get away back!" Uncle Rob hollered. "Now, get in behind, Butch."

While Finn stood confused at the scene, the dogs edged closer to the ewe. At last, they had her steady and on her own.

"Bring her lambs here," Uncle Rob said to Finn.

A wave of confusion swept over the boy. What lambs? Where?

"The newborns! The twins. There!" Uncle Rob gave a quick gesture. Finn set off towards the lambs, dodging clumps of sheep poo pellets scattered among the grass and wildflowers. "Ease up! Don't scare them!"

Bleating, the lambs wobbled to their feet. Soon Finn had one tucked awkwardly under each arm.

"Good," said his uncle. "Set 'em down near their mum. I've given her an injection to calm her down. She's got a third lamb coming. But she's having trouble."

The ewe was lying on her side. Nearby, the dogs crouched, silent.

At that moment Finn saw the rear end of the sheep. Something was poking out. He stared, horrified.

It was the slimy head of another lamb.

"I'll have to pull it out," said Uncle Rob.

Finn's mouth dropped. His stomach churned.

But his uncle gently drew the lamb out into the fresh morning air. It gave a tiny sound and then toppled as it tried to stand.

"A runt," said Uncle Rob, wiping his hands. "The mum's only got two teats, so the twins will be okay, but not this little one."

"What's a runt?" asked Finn.

"A weakling. Most of them die."

Finn's eyes widened.

"But I need this one," added his uncle. Worry lines appeared on his forehead. "I need all the lambs. There have been too many bad years recently. The price of wool is better now than it's been for a long time, so I need all of these lambs to survive."

Finn nodded, his eyes fixed on the tiny creature in his uncle's broad, tanned arms. It looked so helpless.

"I'll look after it," Finn said.

Uncle Rob raised his head and looked at Finn with a curious expression.

"I had a dog back home," Finn went on. "I got him as a puppy."

"Did you now? What did you call him?"

"Taco." The name stuck in his throat, and Finn coughed to cover his pain and embarrassment. "I cared for him really well," he added.

"Righto. The runt's all yours. You'll need to build a yard with hay bales up near the house. I'll show you what to feed the lamb."

"How ... do you feed it?" It was a question that hadn't entered Finn's head.

"You need a bottle with a teat and special milk. You also need a strong arm. Lambs suck so hard they almost suck the teat off the bottle!" Uncle Rob drew his mouth into a gruff smile. "And if you take this job on, you have to stick to it. No pulling out halfway. No telling me tomorrow or the next day you've changed your mind."

Finn took the lamb in his arms. "I won't," he said.

"So," said his uncle, opening the truck door, "the mum sheep's okay. The twins are okay, and hopefully this little critter will be okay, too."

Finn made a silent promise to himself that this little lamb would survive.

Back up at the house, Finn placed her in an old tub, padded with towels, and shut her in the laundry while he set about making a yard.

Chapter 4

Hero

Finn struggled to breathe the first time he entered the hay barn. The strong smell of dry grass overwhelmed him. And the sudden scuttling of a mouse sent him reeling in alarm. His foot landed in a blob of chicken poo.

He stamped to flick off the muck and muttered, "I'm *not* a country kid!" Just then, from the laundry, came a bleating sound.

"Okay, okay," he sighed.

After an hour of lugging large, prickly bales of hay, Finn stood back and viewed the yard he'd fenced off by stacking the blocks. His uncle nodded when he saw it, and then he showed Finn how to make up the lamb's milk formula.

Over dinner that night, Uncle Rob said, "It's not a good idea to get too attached to a weak runt. Sometimes, they don't survive. So, it might be best not to give it a name."

But Finn had already named her Hero. He couldn't wait to tell his mum.

Day followed day. The wind blew hard, the sun shone, or it rained. But in all weather, Finn cared for little Hero. If it was a fine day, he would put her out in the hay-yard to let her romp about. In cold or wet weather, he kept her in the laundry. The only thing he didn't enjoy was cleaning up her messes.

As the days passed, Hero grew stronger. Finn helped Uncle Rob dig out pesky weeds, check the water troughs and fill potholes in the farm tracks.

But at night, after Finn and his mum had chatted on the phone, his thoughts flew back to Taco. He was sure Mrs Abara was looking after him. And maybe Taco already had a new lead. Finn hoped so. He couldn't bear to think of anything happening to his beloved dog. He missed Taco so much.

Watching Uncle Rob with Butch and Mack didn't make it easier. Finn's insides tightened with longing. How he longed to play with the dogs. To run his fingers through their fur. To scratch behind their ears. To call, "Fetch the ball, Mack!"

But then he'd remember his uncle's words: *"Stop! Not too close. They're working dogs, not playthings."* And he'd shove his hands in his pockets as his heart sank.

So, Finn turned his attention to Hero. When the lamb bleated in her little high-pitched, rat-a-tat way, Finn grinned. He scratched her ears, wriggled his fingers through her tufty wool and said, "Pity you can't catch a ball." He laughed at that thought.

Finn didn't realise that tomorrow, there would be nothing to laugh about.

Chapter 5

An Escape!

It all began when Finn's mum phoned that night. She'd had a call from Mrs Abara.

"Has something happened to Taco?" Finn's voice rose.

"No," said his mum. "She wanted to let you know that Taco's doing fine, that's all."

At the news, Finn trembled with mixed emotions. He was glad that Taco was happy. But … did that mean Taco had forgotten him? A sob rose in Finn's throat.

"I know," said his mum, soothingly.

Finn woke the next morning with a sick, sorrowful feeling in his stomach. At breakfast, he stared dismally at the flakes of cereal floating in the bowl of milk.

His uncle's phone rang.

"Yeah, sure, Max," Uncle Rob said. "Be up there soon. I'll bring extra rope." He turned to Finn. "I have to go out for a while. I need to help a neighbour up the road with a bogged tractor. You can come if you want."

"No, it's okay," said Finn. "I'll feed Her–" Finn broke off. "I mean, the lamb."

"Will you be all right?"

"Yes."

Finn fed Hero in the yard and rinsed the bottle. It felt odd being on his own. For a while, he just wandered about, kicking stones.

Behind the barn, he found an old, faded tennis ball. Finn tossed it from one hand to the other and wondered when his mum would come to collect him.

He missed his mum. Other thoughts crept into his head, too, worried thoughts about starting a new school and meeting new kids.

Hero bleated from her yard.

"You want to play catch, Hero?" To cheer himself up, Finn tossed the ball into the yard and scrambled over the bales to see what Hero would do. She sniffed the ball. And then walked away. With a gloomy shrug, Finn picked up the ball and pitched it as hard as he could out of the yard, towards the trees.

A dog barked. Finn froze.

Had one of the dogs got the ball? Clambering over a bale, he rushed to find the dogs.

Sometimes, when Uncle Rob wasn't working them, he tied Butch and Mack up with long leads near their kennels to rest. But he'd left in a hurry that morning, leaving them free.

Mack had the ball.

"Here, boy," said Finn, running up to the dog. "Drop the ball. Drop it."

Mack turned his head to one side, a keen look in his eye.

"Come on, Mack. Drop the ball."

Finn paused, then approached slowly, with one hand stretched out. Nearby, Butch barked with excitement and began to dart back and forth as if he was on springs.

"Drop!"

Mack lowered his head, tail wagging. The ball fell from his mouth.

"Good boy." But before Finn had a chance to grab the ball, Butch dashed up like a streak of lightning, snatched the ball and ran off.

"Butch! Stop!"

Butch kept running and Mack joined in the game.

"Stop, Butch! Drop the ball."

Amazingly, he did.

This time, Finn was faster. "Ha!" Triumphantly, he held the slobbery ball up high.

The two dogs stood poised before him, alert and ready for more fun.

"No." Finn shook his head, again remembering his uncle's words.

But then, then ... he also remembered Taco and the games they had played. How he'd laughed and romped with his dog. How Taco had skidded and pounced and trotted back with the ball. And there were Mack and Butch, staring wide-eyed and prancing before him.

Finn took a breath. "Just once, then," he said, and meant it.

He threw the ball.

Butch snaffled the ball and raced off. Barking, Mack gave chase as Butch headed back towards the house … and the hay-bale yard.

"No!" shrieked Finn. "Stop! Stop!"

But Butch leapt over the fence. And down went a bale. It toppled inwards, startling Hero.

The lamb jumped. In a flash, she was out of the yard and scampering away towards the paddocks.

Chapter 6

A Rescue

It took a moment for Finn to react. Then he tore after her. Hero had grown into a sturdy lamb, and she could run.

Finn needed to command the dogs, but he didn't know the exact words or whistles that his uncle used. Instead, he flailed his arms and cried, "Get the lamb! Stop the lamb!"

The dogs took off. But Hero dodged and skittered, around rocks, down slopes, and along the farm track. Puffing, Finn tried to hedge her towards a rocky crevice, but she was too fast. Terrified, she scampered away. Finn raced after her, red-faced and sweating. There was a lump in his throat so big he could hardly swallow. He had to get the lamb. He *had* to.

But the dogs weren't helping.

Angrily, he spun around. "Butch! Mack! Get back. Go back!" They paused. Then they took off after Hero again. Finn flung his arms in the air. But then, ahead, he saw a sharp bend in the track. If Hero slowed down …

Pushing hard, Finn sped up. At the bend, the lamb halted. "Now," muttered Finn.

But as if she'd understood, Hero sprang over the edge of the track and scuttled down the slope.

"NO!" screamed Finn. Directly below was a fast-flowing stream.

Finn looked around wildly for help. A broken, leafy branch lay at the base of a tree. Thinking fast, and with only a moment to judge his aim, Finn hurled the branch towards the river so it landed with a thump in front of Hero.

Hero pulled up. Then, immediately, she spun around and headed in the opposite way, back up the slope.

That was when Finn hurled himself at her. Hero wriggled and squirmed, but Finn clung on. Butch and Mack crouched nearby, panting, their tongues lolling to one side.

Breathless, Finn dragged himself back up to the yard.

Then, in a frenzy, he replaced the fallen bale and set Hero down. He was tying up the dogs just as a flurry of dust rose from the driveway and Uncle Rob returned.

Chapter 7

Mum's Surprise

Dinner time came and still the question hammered in Finn's head. Should he tell Uncle Rob what had happened that day or not?

"More mashed potato?" asked his uncle.

"No, thanks."

"Not hungry? You've hardly touched your food."

Finn's ears warmed. The words pushed towards his mouth until finally he blurted, "The lamb escaped today."

Uncle Rob paused. His brow crinkled. "Oh? But she's back now."

"Yes. I got her back."

"And she's doing well, thanks to you. She's strong enough to join the other lambs." Uncle Rob put down his fork. "Anything else you've got to say?"

And then the words came out. Finn stared at the tabletop, listening to them echoing in his head. "I'm sorry, Uncle."

Uncle Rob reached out and laid a hand on Finn's shoulder.

"It's all right, son," he said. "You made a mistake. But you fixed it. It's all right."

Finn raised his head and released a breath. A wavering smile played about his lips.

"And guess what?" his uncle continued. "Your mum's coming tomorrow."

Finn raised his eyebrows. "I didn't know that."

"She wanted to wait until she was sure about everything. But I think she's got news for you," Uncle Rob continued.

When the next day came, Finn's mum hugged him so tightly he could hardly breathe. They both laughed.

"So, not only do I have a car," his mum said, with a grin and a proud waggle of her head, "but I have a job at an aged-care centre. *And* a house for us as well, about an hour from here. I think you're going to love it, Finn."

"Wow, that sounds great, Mum!" said Finn. Turning towards his uncle, he added, "So, we can visit you?"

"Sure can."

"What's more," his mum continued, "the house has got a backyard. Big enough for a …"

With that, she opened the car door and lifted out a puppy. A beautiful, fluffy black-and-white border collie.

Finn gasped. "For me?" he said, his eyes filling with tears.

"He's all yours, Finn," said his mum. "Your uncle heard about a litter born nearby, and how the puppies were ready to leave their mother. So, I picked this little one up on the way. What do you think?"

Finn couldn't speak. He hugged the puppy, snuggled his face into its soft fur and rubbed its velvety ears.

"He's lovely, Mum," he stammered. "Thank you. And thanks, Uncle Rob."

"You'll have to think of a name, now," said his uncle.

Finn smiled. "I think I've already got one."

"What's that, then?" said his uncle.

"Robbie," said Finn.

A slow grin spread across his uncle's face and his eyes lit up. "Sounds all right to me," he said. "Yep. Sounds all right to me."